A NEW WAY TO DIE. A NEW WAY TO LIVE.

INTERSTELLAR
FUNERAL

JAY HALL

Interstellar Funeral

bettercalljayhall@gmail.com

ISBN: 978-1-0690945-5-1

Printed in Canada

First Edition: March 2025

Appeal

Being a writer in this day and age is harder than ever. While we may not have the challenges of using a typewriter, AI and other threats continue to make it challenging for writers to break through.

I ask, if you enjoyed this story, please tell people online, in-person, and on review sites like Fable, Goodreads, and most importantly, Amazon. If you work at a movie studio, please tell the decision makers! And if you liked the story enough to want to read more of my works in the future, please consider signing up for my mailing list at projectsbyjay.com. I'll be releasing side plot shorts, poems, and other wordplay connected to this story regularly.

It has been my dream for quite some time to write for a living. I love podcasting: betterpodcast.live, and acting is a lot of fun, but writing is my first love.

I know so many authors who tell incredible stories that are never seen. One day, I'd love to start a publishing house for those that traditional publishers won't pay attention to. For now though, I would appreciate you spreading the word about this novella.

Thank you.

* * *

Jay

PART ONE

The Return of Oliver Owen

A faint hum from overhead fluorescent lights, buzzing like angry bees, filled Oliver Owen's ears as he paced the cramped green room. His heart hammered against his ribs, each beat drowning out the faint audio playing from TV monitors delivering carefully crafted marketing messages to the audience of millions he was about to address. Even his competition took out ads for the segment featuring thinly veiled jabs in Owen's direction.

Great, he thought to himself. *Of all our advancements in the last few decades, snarky commercials are still a thing. Progress does indeed have steep limits.*

He was minutes away from his first appearance in five years, the first time he would face the world since a catastrophic accident that had taken 288 lives in a blink that lasted forever in his mind's eye. It was a day of great tragedy that instantly washed away his decades of contribution to health, policy, space exploration, and economic balance.

In the weeks following the accident, the pervasive grief

of the families was palpable as they recounted their losses in interviews across the internet. Amidst their tears and shared grief, a single, burning question echoed—*why had Owen falsely assured them of the mission's safety?*

Years later, the answer emerged: a disgruntled employee, consumed by bitterness, had sabotaged the mission, seeking to destroy Oliver's life, career, and reputation—although the deaths were an unintended consequence. His confession, a self-recorded suicide video posted on YouTube, came years too late for Oliver. It would be published and shared, but relegated to the bottom of news websites because, in the media's view, Oliver was no longer relevant. At that point, he hadn't shown his face in public for a couple of years and rumours swirled he had lost his mind.

Suicide would ease that former employee's guilt, but the answers did little to ease Oliver's. He was expected, as a man of intellect, to always be twelve steps ahead, anticipating and planning for every contingency with unnerving accuracy. Even his most innocent human moments and gaffes were dissected and scrutinized by independent media outlets. The accident was anything but innocent, so the world turned on him as conspiracies took hold of the zeitgeist.

Despite the careful styling of his wavy, dark hair and

the tailored navy suit meant to convey confidence, Oliver felt unsteady—like he stood on the edge of a clay cliff, looking down into a pit with no end in sight.

He braced himself against a cool concrete wall, palms splayed out, forehead gently tapping the rough surface. Horrific images flashed unbidden: the shuttle bursting into flames, passengers screaming as the expanse of space choked them, flames licking the hull before it tore apart, and the absolute silence afterward—so total, so final.

This movie had been playing on repeat in his mind for years. His work was the only escape from these tormenting visions, but even he couldn't work without pause.

His breath caught in his throat, coming in sharp, shallow gasps. He clenched his teeth, silently reciting the breathing exercises his fifth or sixth therapist had taught him. *Focus. Inhale, exhale.*

Once again, the last words of the pilot from his shuttle's radio echoed through every cell and tissue of his mind. "Tell my family I—"

The explosion would cut his message short. The obvious assumption was that the astronaut wanted his family to know that he loved them, but Oliver couldn't reconcile the unfinished message. Perhaps the man wanted to say *cherish* or convey that he was thankful for them. Perhaps he harboured a secret that demanded revelation.

He was robbed of his chance to finish that sentence, dying a moment too soon in the most horrifying of ways. That pilot's name was Commander Paul Comber, and he was the inspiration behind the theme of today's interview.

A young production assistant pensively peered around the doorframe, obviously intimidated by his presence. "Mr. Owen?" she asked softly. "We're going live in one minute."

Oliver struggled to blink himself back into the present. He attempted a smile, but his clammy skin gave him away. "Are you alright, Mr. Owen?"

"I'm fine," he managed, even though a shakiness laced his words.

She didn't look convinced. "Are you sure, sir?"

He nodded briskly. "I'm sure. Thank you."

She hesitated for a moment and then slipped away, standing just outside of the room. Oliver closed his eyes for one last moment, inhaled deeply, and imagined he exhaled every fear with their hooks in him. By the time he stood upright, he wore the gentle mask he'd perfected over decades in the public eye.

When he emerged onto the dimly lit set, the crew stopped and stared—some with disgust, others with that look on their faces Oliver aptly called, *what can he do for me?* Being one of the world's richest men, his relationships with most were defined by his ability to provide some kind of value.

A solitary camera tracked him as he made his way to the two chairs perched center stage. Katie Colter, a veteran reporter known for her incisive interviews, rose to greet him as the crew watched on. Her handshake was firm, her eyes shrewd, and then she gestured for him to take his seat. Between them, two glasses of water sat on a small table, capturing glints of overhead studio lights.

"Mr. Owen," Katie began, her voice raw and tone, suspicious. "It's been half a decade since the world has seen or heard from you. You reached out to me personally, saying you've been working on something you'd like to share—something you believe will change the world. But before we get to that, let's address the elephant in the room."

Oliver's throat tightened. He knew the question would come. Of course she'd start there; the shuttle tragedy seemed to be the only reason the world still remembered his name.

Katie clasped her hands in her lap. "Five years ago, you pioneered commercial space travel. Thousands of people clamoured to be among the first to leave Earth's orbit. But your second year of shuttle flight ended in devastating tragedy, killing all 288 souls on board." She paused, letting the weight of her words sit for a moment. "Why should anyone trust you again?"

He felt the eyes of the world bearing down on him. The same images he'd just tried to bury pressed into his consciousness, and he had to force himself not to retreat. He glanced at the floor briefly, drawing in a fortifying breath. After a moment, he steadied himself with a slight nod.

"It was the worst day of my life," Oliver admitted, voice husky. "I haven't been in public because I… didn't know how to face it. So many families were left broken, and I owe them more than I can ever repay." He paused, throat tightening again. "But I can't pretend that day didn't happen. I can't bring those people back. All I can do is devote myself to making sure the future is brighter—safer. My only goal now is to contribute something meaningful to humanity again. And that's why I'm here tonight."

Katie pressed him further. "Some would say you abandoned the families of the victims, that you showed cowardice instead of taking responsibility the moment you needed to. How do you respond?"

"Sometimes the world—your own thoughts are too heavy." He said as he gripped the arms of the chair tighter. "I left my people to handle the aftermath because I was in no place mentally or physically to help anyone. Whether that was the right call, I don't know. I can see how people would describe it as cowardly. But, I couldn't sleep, eat, or think without guilt collapsing down on me for months. In that state, I felt like I could only do more harm. I...I didn't know how to face them—or myself."

Katie's eyes were unyielding, her tone just as hard. "It's been five years, Mr. Owen. Why now? Should we assume your guilt is gone?"

He swallowed, feeling the heat of shame crawling up his neck. "God, no. It takes everything in me to not let that guilt consume me anytime I take a breath. That will never change, so I decided to channel it."

"Channel your guilt?" Katie asked skeptically.

"I've been working all this time, trying to find a way not just to atone, but to truly help people who feel powerless in the face of loss. I called you here because I want the world to know what I've been doing—and who it's for. I've been calling the project Interstellar Funeral."

Katie shifted in her seat. "Interstellar Funeral," she repeated, ensuring no viewer missed the unusual phrasing. "Sounds like something out of science fiction. What exactly do you mean by that?"

"Hasn't everything I've ever done sounded like science fiction at first?" Oliver looked down at his hands, momentarily gathering his thoughts. "I know this might seem unthinkable at first," he said, voice low but steady.

"But in the last decade, the world has changed drastically. Burial space is at a premium and that has led to thousands of cases of body snatching—so many that it's become as commonplace in the news cycle as criticisms of politicians. Cremation is at an all-time low because of religious zealots convincing people it's the gateway to hell. The last two pandemics were handled so inhumanely, bodies dropped into the ocean by the thousands to become fish food or burned. More than that, people—people who know they're dying—are often left with too few dignified options. Especially when they're in pain or can't afford sophisticated end-of-life care. They lay in a cold, unapologetic and noisy room, with people checking on them every few minutes to see if they're dead yet. They're no longer people. The toe tag is practically tied the day they find out they're dying. I saw it with my mom and frankly, I've seen it in every hospital I've ever funded."

Katie cut in. "And you're going to solve all of those problems?"

He glanced up, meeting Katie's gaze. "I want to offer something different. A final journey that isn't bound by Earth's limitations, a journey that could mean something. I want to do it in a way that might help us learn more about who we are, where we come from, and maybe even where we're going. That's the heart of Interstellar Funeral: a chance for individuals to die peacefully while literally reaching for the stars."

For the first time, Katie's hardened expression seemed to waver. Still, she wasn't done pressing him. "You say 'die peacefully.' But why should anyone trust you to handle that responsibility when your last space endeavour ended with the least peaceful deaths imaginable?"

Oliver inhaled sharply. "Trust can't be demanded; it has to be earned. I know this won't erase the past. But I'm determined to make Interstellar Funeral safer and more meaningful than anything we've tried before. One mission out of hundreds failed. Yes, it was my fault. I should have watched over the project with more consideration for possibilities similar to what happened. Yes. But should we then stop trying to make a difference? Over the past five years, Owen Industries has made breakthroughs in metallurgy and propulsion that we've tested exhaustively. This time, we're not carrying tourists chasing thrills. We're guiding people who've made a conscious choice to spend their final days or moments in an environment that might inspire them—and us. Plus, I'll be supervising every ship build personally."

A flicker of genuine curiosity sparked in Katie's eyes. "So what makes these 'funeral pods' feasible? How does this project differ from traditional end-of-life care… or from a more conventional space program? And to add to that; how will you have the time to supervise this all?"

Oliver exhaled slowly, relieved to shift to a topic that was equal parts inspiring and redemptive. "We've developed a new metal alloy that's cost-effective and extremely resilient under harsh conditions—heat, radiation, and micrometeoroids. These single-occupancy pods have advanced telecommunications systems, so the occupant can speak with loved ones on Earth or companion travellers in other pods. They contain intravenous hydration and sedation, with the option of a barbiturate if they choose to end their journey. For comfort, we have a technology called Relief Suppression, eliminating the need for a restroom and even restlessness. Each pod has solar power converters, a molecular hydrogen fuel system, and even a specialized camera array —adapted from older NASA and James Webb Telescope designs—to send back data as it travels deeper into space. For the first time ever, we'll have human involvement in deep space travel."

Katie's brows knitted, a mixture of skepticism and fascination. "But who would be the first to do this?"

Oliver's voice gentled. "Beth Jenkins and Chase Melnyk—two individuals facing terminal illnesses. They approached me through our Death with Dignity outreach.

Together, we've been refining this idea. Their launch is in three weeks."

Katie paused; if she needed to absorb the quickness of the revelation, she was sure her viewers did as well. "You're saying, in twenty-one days or so, you'll send two people—willingly, knowingly—into space to die on their own—"

"Terms," Oliver added. "Die on their own terms."

"Will they be doing this together?"

"They'll be able to communicate with each other, but after much deliberation we decided to make the pods fit for one."

Katie's expression was skeptical but curious. "Single-occupancy pods... Why would anyone want that?"

"We live in the year 2056," Oliver said, his voice taking on more purpose. "People expect better options for all aspects of their lives—even their death. My company's solution is to let people explore the stars in their final moments, up to six months, if they choose. There are plenty of reasons to do this physically alone, but they'll never really be alone. Memories and communication with others are at their fingertips. Think about it, people die alone in hospital beds all the time. Sadly, it's a fate most seniors must confront."

Katie let the moment linger before leaning forward.

"And cost?"

"That's been one of my biggest concerns," Oliver replied, shoulders squaring. "I've arranged for an $8,000 government subsidy for anyone who chooses this option. Additionally, I've pledged to donate half my personal fortune annually to sponsor those who can't afford it, ensuring finances aren't the deciding factor in whether someone can die on their own terms. But we start with two people out of pocket and continue from there."

Katie studied him, no longer cold but contemplative. "I have to admit, Mr. Owen, this is…a lot to process. Do you believe this will change our understanding of death?"

He thought of the families he'd failed. "I believe everyone should have the right to choose how they face the inevitable. If nothing else, this will offer a more humane passing. But I also hope the data these pods collect will help us understand the cosmos better. Imagine one day stumbling upon something that shifts our perception of life itself and a human being there to witness it. Not just witness, but convey! That alone is worth it."

Katie looked to the camera and then back at Oliver. "We're nearly out of time. Mr. Owen, is there anything you'd like to say to those watching tonight—especially to the families who may still blame you for what happened?"

Oliver drew in a breath, gaze drifting momentarily

toward the studio's darkened corners. The silence grew awkward as he carefully considered his words and pushed his panic down through his toes.

"Mr. Owen?" Katie pushed.

Finally, he looked into the camera, his voice grew warm and resolute—a vulnerability shining through.

"When I was younger, I believed legacy was about conquest, about building empires, having more than most. Then, as I grew older, I thought legacy was about changing the world. After the accident, I learned the hard way that life is fleeting, and our true legacy is the love we share, the lives we touch, and the hope we pass on. We don't know what happens when we die or if any of this really means anything, but I do know that our actions and our values mean everything to those we affect."

He took another moment to think. "We're in an age where people have lost faith in each other. But we can't let the fractures between us define our future. We have to hold on to the things that bring us joy and hope—friends, family, the wonder of the unknown and our ability to discover more. And for those in pain, we can't ignore their suffering. I once tried to be a hero by conquering space; now, all I want is to help people see that they're not alone in their fear of the end but together, with care, we can find ways to truly make life worth living and death worthy of a life well lived. I just want love to be the last thing as many people as possible can experience. Nothing more, nothing less. I think we can all agree that a little more love would go a long way. With Interstellar Funeral, people's final moments are filled with love while their final days are filled with wonder. It won't be for everyone but for those with wonder and love in their hearts… what a way to leave this plane of existence."

A hush fell over the set. Katie swallowed, visibly moved, before turning to face the camera. "Thank you, Mr. Owen. I'm sure we're about to see how people feel about this concept."

As the lights dimmed and the red recording light blinked off, Oliver felt a tight weight lift from his shoulders —just a little. There would be critics, yes, but for the first time since the tragedy five years ago, he believed there might be a path forward. A path toward redemption—and perhaps, toward giving the human race something they so desperately needed: hope, even in the end.

PART TWO

Beth's Goodbyes

Beth closed her eyes as the nurse gently wheeled her into the grand ballroom of the Wellshire Event Center. A rolling wave of applause greeted her, and when she opened her eyes, she was bathed in soft golden light that caught the glitter and feathers adorning her friends and family.

Swirling silhouettes in fringed dresses and pinstriped suits captured her excitement as her eyes darted from one lavish outfit to another. It was exactly the sort of 1920s-themed party she always dreamed of having since she became obsessed with the era in her roaring 20s—jazzy saxophone music mingling with laughter, the crisp sound of a snare drum keeping time while people sipped mocktails topped with foam and cherries.

She couldn't stand on her own most days—the treatments had exhausted her, and she'd had too many falls recently—but that didn't bother her in the slightest today. Oliver had arranged for her to have the most tech'd out wheelchair available so that she would be comfortable as the center of attention at her celebration.

Marquee letters reading Beth's Big Band Blowout shone

above a small stage, where a live band played a snappy tune reminiscent of the era. Every face turned toward her, and the glow in their eyes was like a collective embrace.

Her seven-year-old great-nephew draped a feather boa over her shoulders, making Beth feel a bit like a film star from a nearly forgotten era at this point. Her granddaughter handed her a decorative fan with a custom printed picture of her family. Then, shuffling up to her with as much of a skip in her step as she could muster, Beth's long-time friend and bridge partner pressed a fascinator onto her impeccably styled grey locks.

Even though she was 63 and feeling weaker with every passing day, tonight she felt very much alive.

Beth spent the next hour receiving kisses on the cheek, warm hugs, and earnest well-wishes. Distant cousins she hadn't seen in years showed up in fringed dresses, while her old college roommate—wearing a jaunty fedora—slipped Beth a locket containing a tiny photograph of the two of them from decades ago when they were young and fetching. Her dear friend Shayna, all dolled up in a satin drop-waist gown, regaled her with stories from their youth. "Remember when Tommy Drake tried to pick you up at the mall and you told him—"

Beth cut in, matching Shayna's words and tone, "—you're cute, but so are puppies and my poodle doesn't walk around the mall with his fly down."

They cackled. "I've never seen someone's face change that many shades of red so quickly."

Beth laughed until tears welled the corners of her eyes. "Tommy never wanted to hit on me after that," she managed in between breathless beats of laughter. She swallowed down a lump in her throat, pressing the memories of growing up with Shayna close to her heart. This was precisely what the night was about: love, laughter, and her irresistible zest for life.

As she moved around the room in her wheelchair, Beth found herself bombarded by affectionate tributes. A group of friends performed a short jazz dance, complete with flapper costumes and parasols, all to celebrate her spirit and the fierce optimism she'd shown throughout her illness. Meanwhile, a line of her neighbours formed near the punch table, waiting patiently for a moment to share a memory and heartfelt goodbyes. Beneath shimmering Art déco decorations, dozens of people were determined to let Beth know just how deeply she was cherished without letting sorrow win the day.

Eventually, the band quieted, and the overhead lights dimmed. A large screen rolled down at the far end of the ballroom, flickering to life with the only departure from theme—A Thousand Years by Christina Perri, Beth's favourite song. A montage of colourful images played.

It started with photos of Beth as a baby, swaddled in a powder-blue blanket in her mother's arms—her eyes already bright with curiosity. The images flickered, showing scenes from Beth's childhood: a little girl proudly riding her bike without training wheels. The video skipped ahead to her teenage years: wide smiles, silly poses with her best friends, and the day she won a rap battle at a bar she and Shayna had snuck into.   A hush fell over the crowd when pictures of Jesse appeared on the screen— Beth's beloved, tall, built like a boxer, smiling husband, with his arm draped over her shoulders at the beach. She had twelve years with the man of her dreams before an accident relegated him to a memory burned into her mind.

Then came short video clips: Beth, heavily pregnant, painting a nursery for baby Amy; Beth singing lullabies in a rocking chair; Beth and Amy dancing in the kitchen to old Spice Girls songs, their hair in matching messy buns.

Watching her life unfold in front of her—pixel by pixel, memory by memory—Beth felt a warmth spreading through her body.

Tears slipped down her cheeks as the images continued: Amy's first day of school, Beth's many volunteer projects, family holidays, birthdays, anniversaries. And more recent moments, too: photos of

Beth after her diagnosis, still wearing her sunny smile, surrounded by friends who refused to leave her side.

Each photo or video brought a Great Flood of memories, a testament to a life well-lived, even when her illness attempted to rob her of her shine.

Her heart ached with gratitude, and she couldn't stop the tears from flowing. She clutched the hands of Amy, standing behind her wheelchair, silently thanking her for bringing her to this moment. Soft murmurs from the crowd punctuated the video, many of them swiping at their own eyes as the collage of memories reached its finale—a final video in slow motion: Beth, kicking off her slippers and doing the Mom Dance with a huge grin on her face. This video was particularly poignant because she had just been told they could no longer do anything to save her. What a thing to celebrate with vigour.

A swell of applause rose as the screen went dark. Beth dabbed her eyes with a handkerchief, lifting her face to the crowd. In that moment, she felt an indescribable wholeness, a sense that all her joys and sorrows had converged here, in this single, beautiful celebration.

A few moments later, a gentle voice came through the speakers. Amy stood on the small stage, microphone in hand, dark hair tumbling in soft waves down her back. She looked radiant in a beaded 1920s-inspired gown, her posture poised yet brimming with affection.

"Hi, everyone," Amy said, her voice a little shaky. She cleared her throat. "Thank you for coming tonight to celebrate my mom—Beth Jenkins. A woman who's always believed in the beauty of life, no matter how tough things got."

Amy turned her gaze to her mother. "Mom, I remember being a little girl and writing down, in the most dramatic way possible, the list of exactly what I needed in a man to be happy. I was twelve, and it was a list filled with important things—like needing him to be taller than me so I could wear high heels, or that he had to like dogs because I was desperate for a puppy." She paused, waiting for a wave of laughter to settle in the back of the room. "And I'll never forget the day I told you about Ian. I could see in your eyes that you remembered that list, even if your memory wasn't so great. Neither was mine. I was twelve, after all. You said the way I spoke about him, you knew, and then you pulled the list out of your box of keepsakes, the one dad gave you on your wedding night, and you asked me so sweetly if Ian measured up to that starry-eyed dream from my twelve-year-old imagination."

People chuckled, some glancing over to a tall man standing near the stage—clearly Ian, exuding a quiet confidence in his tailored vest and slacks. Amy's eyes found him, her expression brightening even further. "Sure enough, Mom, he checked all the boxes. So you hugged me and gave me that short but eternally memorable speech about love. You told me to never forget the magic and wonder I felt. That if a love truly makes you feel more alive and if you can be with him as you are when no one's around, that's how you know it's real."

Beth nodded, recalling the day well—Amy's face flushed with excitement at finding Ian. Beth had offered her patented mixture of motherly concern and unwavering support. *I was so proud of you*, she thought.

Amy took a moment to steady her voice, then smiled. "And now, Mom, we wanted to do something special. As you prepare for a journey of a lifetime, all fifty-six of us here tonight recorded personal video messages for you to take in your pod. Also, everyone here opened their homes to Owen Industries so they could install their fancy, high-tech communications devices. That way, even when you're out there among the stars, you'll still hear our voices, and we can hear yours whenever you want. You will truly never be alone."

An emotional hush fell over the guests; a few sniffles broke the stillness. "We all love you so much, Mom," Amy said, her eyes brimming with tears. "You've always given us the very best of yourself. Tonight is our chance to show you that we're with you every step of the way—even if your path eventually leads beyond Earth." She paused for a moment. "What a surreal thing to say."

The applause that followed was rampant but classy. Beth raised her trembling hands to press against her heart, wordlessly thanking them for this precious gift.

For the next half hour, the ballroom buzzed with renewed energy. The band kicked back into gear, and slices of a tall, Art déco-themed cheesecake were passed around —Cheesecake Factory's lemon meringue, Beth's favourite.

People danced the Charleston, took pictures as the vintage themed drone buzzed around the room, and lingered by Beth's side to share final private words.

Every so often, Beth's gaze would flick toward Amy and Ian. The way they interacted—comfortable but loving, always with an ease in each other's presence—filled her with warmth and peace.

Eventually, as the clock edged toward ten, Beth grew tired. Amy and Ian approached Beth together, hands held firmly, the spectacle of love glistening in their eyes.

"Mom," Amy said softly, "we've got to head to the Owen Industries compound for your final preparations soon. Are you ready?"

Beth gave a small nod, smiling despite the sadness tugging at her heart. "I am." She glanced at the party still whirling around her, the laughter and music underscoring each goodbye. "I'm taking every memory with me," she whispered, grasping Amy's hand.

Ian crouched beside her wheelchair while Amy stood close, one hand lightly resting on her mother's shoulder. Beth patted Ian's broad arm. "Sienna have raised you right," she said, her voice full of approval. "And while I've treasured getting to know her, I have a question about that book your father left for you before he passed. I'm curious…Did he write anything that might help an old lady like me in this moment?"

Ian's face grew thoughtful. "My dad never got to see me grow up—he died shortly after I was born. But I've read his lessons a thousand times. He wrote lots about love, about resilience, about letting people be who they need to be." He drew a slow breath, locking eyes with Beth. "He said you should never ask someone to grieve, process, or face heartbreak on your terms. You have to let them feel what they need to feel, even if you don't understand it. Just be there for them, and celebrate their joys."

Amy leaned in and whispered to her, "It was that chapter of Beck's book that helped me find peace with your decision."

"Is that so?"

"It took me a minute to accept this, as you know, but I'm so happy I did."

Beth felt tears welling again as she tapped Amy's hand and looked back towards Ian. "That's… such a special lesson that too few learn."

"And it's exactly what we're doing for you," Ian continued. "You want to be the first woman to have an Interstellar Funeral. That's a huge deal! And it's right because it's your choice. You got time with everyone you love. You get to try something no other human has. And you're doing it all on your own terms—painful as it may be for the rest of us to let you go. But I think it's beautiful. And perfect."

Beth smiled so big she squinted, her voice trembling slightly. "Thank you, Ian. I wish I could have met your father. He must have been quite the man to steal your mother's heart."

"She wished she could be here, but Spencer couldn't find a flight that worked. She did get the communication device installed in her home as well. Your Scrabble games shall endure!"

"Thank Sienna for me, will ya? And thank you both." She glanced between Ian and Amy, her eyes full of pride. "You two make a wonderful pair. Promise me you'll keep dancing through life, no matter what songs the world plays next."

Amy laughed through her tears. "We promise, Mom."

The final notes of a jaunty jazz tune played as Beth's wheelchair moved towards the door. Amy and Ian carefully guided her through the crowd, with everyone stepping aside in a wave of gentle applause and heartfelt goodbyes. Cameras flashed; more kisses and hugs followed. All the children in her family lined up to plant kisses on her cheeks, and friends pressed keepsakes into her hands. Ribbons and small confetti rained down. When the doors closed behind them, Beth felt as though her entire being was fuelled by love.

Outside, a sleek, silver Owen Industries HyperVan waited to take them to the next phase of her journey. As she sat inside, Beth looked at her reflection in the tinted window—tears on her cheeks and a spark of excitement in her eyes. Part of her heart broke to leave this world, but another part sang at what lay ahead. Death with dignity had never been more peaceful or hopeful, and she was to be the first of two.

She glanced one last time at the doors of the venue, the muffled sound of live jazz just barely reaching her ears, and whispered to herself, "Thank you, everyone. I'll see you among the stars."

With that, the van pulled away from the curb and sailed

into the air, carrying Beth, Amy, and Ian toward Owen Industries—and toward a final adventure that would make Beth Jenkins the first woman in history to greet eternity from the vastness of space.

PART THREE

Chase's Goodbyes

Chase stepped carefully out of a vehicle onto the gravel drive of his friend Devon's cabin, a late-morning sun warming his neck as it rose behind him. Devon's home away from home, where they'd spent many years fishing, had seen better days, but still felt like the safest place on earth. Sure, the paint was peeling and that old canoe that sprung a leak decades ago was still laying on its side with long dead grass pressed into the dirt. And yes, some windows looked more like doors on the top level Devon rarely ventured to anymore, but none of that mattered. The memories he and his friends shared in this place meant it could crash down around him and it would still feel like paradise.

He drew in a lungful of pine-scented air as the breeze ruffled his thinning hair and the front door banged open with his five old friends spilling out onto the porch. The sound of their laughter, carefree and loud, rang across the long, empty driveway.

They were the same rowdy wolf pack he'd grown up with, but now they each had deepened laugh lines, softer middles, and various touches of grey threaded through their hair. Yet something in their eyes glowed with the same mischievous spark Chase remembered from their school days.

His struggling heart seemed to beat with a little more enthusiasm at the sight of five grinning faces waiting for him on the front porch. There was something in the air; a whisper that this—one of his last days on Earth—would be one for the ages.

"Look who finally decided to show up!" Kris hollered, swirling a bottle of whiskey with the confidence of a seasoned connoisseur.

Each friend held something up like a prize on display. Devon triumphantly held an old Playstation 5 controller over his head, battered around the edges but still operational after decades. Lincoln, their resident carefree spirit, flashed a mason jar of weed with a mischievous grin. Darius flipped a DVD case in his hands; WrestleMania 17. Ferris, along with everyone else, wore the same faded UNLV sweater, a nostalgic nod to the best time of their lives—childhood friends sharing a dorm and getting into all kinds of trouble. In his hand, Chase's sweater, creased from storage but still in pretty good shape.

At one point, they'd met at the cozy, rustic cabin three times a year, but as they aged and Kris moved across the ocean, their visits became infrequent. This was the first time in six years they were all together again.

"Forgot your walker, old man?" Lincoln teased. "After I'm done with ya, you'll need it just to stand."

"Shut it," Chase shot back, grinning. "These doctors have me on so many drugs, I might just be immune to your homegrown weed."

They all busted out laughing—equal parts relief and joy. It felt good not to tiptoe around the fact that Chase's heart was giving out, that their collective bodies weren't what they once were. The easy camaraderie had always been their greatest strength, and it was alive and well, despite the years.

Inside the cozy A-frame with rustic wooden beams and big windows overlooking the turquoise lake beyond, the place smelled faintly of old wood and the brisk wind off the water. Memories flooded Chase's consciousness: boisterous holiday weekends, impromptu fishing trips with half the group losing rods to the current and angry, stubborn fish, and lazy mornings sipping coffee on the deck as loons called across the still water.

Ferris tossed Chase his sweater. "You do still fit in this, right?"

"Fit is a generous word," Chase said, yanking it over his head, anyway. He patted his slight belly. "I'll probably split a seam if I so much as sneeze. But… worth it."

In the living room, they laid out the day's indulgences. Devon fiddled with the Playstation 5, hooking it up to a large, wall-mounted screen, as Ferris rummaged in a cooler for sodas, mixers, and snacks, and Lincoln got on his knees to roll a joint.

"You better be able to get up without help, Lincoln," Chase ribbed at him. "I don't think any of us are gonna be able to assist you to your feet."

"I'm still in the best shape of anyone in this room," he proclaimed while attempting to shoot up to his feet, quickly losing his balance and falling back onto the couch behind him to the roar of laughter.

"You look like McMahon taking a Stone Cold stunner," Darius proclaimed while grabbing the DVD case and skimming the back cover. "Gentlemen, do you remember the night we first watched this?" he asked, smiling ear to ear. "You guys had a keg in your basement, Kris, and your dad almost caught us—"

"*Almost?*" Kris scoffed, twisting open the whiskey with a satisfying pop. "He watched us on the cameras for like an hour, just didn't say anything until after Stone Cold pinned The Rock. Then he grounded me for two weeks."

Lincoln howled at the memory. "Dude, that was the same night you tried that half-baked pile-driver on me and nearly broke my neck! I was hurting for weeks, so you got what you deserved."

Chase took in the scene with a contented sigh. No one mentioned his failing heart, nor his upcoming one-way trip, courtesy of Owen Industries. At least, not yet.

Instead, they filled the time with recollections of growing up along that lonely rural road where their five families' farms nestled close together. That tight-knit bond had seen them through heartbreak, divorces, military deployments, losing a couple members in their group, and layoffs. Today, it would see them through a final celebration of sorts.

Lincoln finished rolling a near-perfect joint, the sweet scent of cannabis filling the air as he held it up with pride, like Lady Liberty holding her torch.

"Are we still pretending we have the tolerance we did in our teens, or…?" Kris questioned.

"Ah yes, our prime years," Ferris chimed in. "Our biggest worry was whether the girl we liked would notice our severely inflated egos—and questionable cologne."

"Well, that was the biggest worry for most of us. Not Chase, though." Devon stated with a crooked smile. "How many times did the cops get called on you?"

Devon recounted a story that made Chase's cheeks burn with amused embarrassment as the joint was passed around. "Remember that time you and—what was her name, Georgia?—got locked in that EQ3 store in the mall 'cause you *fell asleep* in a display bed? Your mom thought you were abducted when she found your car in the deserted mall parking lot."

"Oh man," Chase groaned, cringing playfully. "It was a fantastic *nap*…until it actually turned into a nap and we woke up to total darkness and realized there was no version of the story that didn't look like breaking and entering."

"Don't forget the best part," Kris said between puffs and coughs. "His mom showed back up at the mall cussing like a sailor after the cops called her. The second she saw the security footage of her little baby boy taking a *trip* to Georgia, she just about ended him."

They all roared. Chase could almost hear his mom's voice echoing through time. He missed her fiery spirit, even when that fire was directed at him.

The late morning turned into late afternoon, with spirits as *high* as they were. The five men giggled like a bunch of teenagers ditching class behind the gym. Devon managed to get his hands on something incredibly rare in 2056—real meat steaks. Coupled with generous portions of sides, the men devoured their meals, stacking the dishes high on the kitchen counter.

A couple of them tried their hand at the vintage PlayStation, hollering as they fumbled through archaic game mechanics and marvelled that they ever found it impressive. A PS5 was no match for ocular implants and mixed reality in 64k. Jokes flew left and right about how Ferris rarely dated in high school because he had found the love of his life early—Lara Croft from the game Tomb Raider.

Their laughter and loud voices echoed through the small cabin, shaking the dust from the rafters.

Eventually though, Kris let his curiosity get the best of him. "Chase, can I ask…why you? Of all the people Oliver Owen could've chosen for this Interstellar Funeral, why an old dog like you?"

"Yeah, I mean, don't they usually pick guys with abs and nice hair? A hot blonde with big boobs and yoga pants for these sorts of things?" Ferris interjected.

"I don't know too many people that look like that when death is a couple of steps behind them," Chase said in a deadpan tone.

A hush settled over the group as their attention shifted to the uncomfortable subject.

He looked down at the swirling amber in his glass. "It's not about *me*, it's about my wrinkles and greys," he said softly, never raising his gaze. "We all know that after a certain age, the world sees us as more of a burden than anything. Been that way a long time—remember back in 2020 when the pandemic started and some folks said, 'So what if old people die? They've had a good run'? An old person's life wasn't worth putting on a mask. That was the first time I realized how people would view me when I got to this age, even though we were all young bucks. Something changed in people—the things they said in their heads could be said for everyone to hear, and it's only gotten worse. Beth and I are the perfect *test run* because if something goes wrong with this new project, folks won't consider it as big a tragedy, like if two people in their 30s were to die or get hurt."

They nodded, each staring off into the distance, not really looking at anything. Ferris gazed through a window. "We used to talk like technology would cure old age," he admitted. "Remember? When we were in our twenties, we'd see some old guy shuffling slowly across the street and be all, 'Come on, Gramps, move it along.' Thought we'd never end up like that."

Devon sighed while slowly shifting in his seat. "Yeah, we were so cocky, so sure we'd never be *boring old people*. Turns out, I enjoy going to bed by 9 p.m. these days—my back thanks me."

"Seriously, though," Kris added, "if youth could

understand that everyone has value—just...*different* value —the world would be a much better place. We might not run marathons anymore, but we've got experience— lessons to share."

Chase let the words sink in. "Exactly," he said softly. "Our generation has so much to offer—every generation does. Oliver Owen knows people ignore seniors, so if anything does go sideways with this first mission, the blowback won't be as bad. But that same logic says it's my turn to show we can still matter, that we have the courage to do something new and groundbreaking. We're not fossils meant to be kept in a museum. Us old-timers are tried, tested, and true trailblazers."

A charged hush followed. Nobody quite knew what to say, so they let the quiet speak for them—a thousand memories playing on their faces, a thousand acknowledgments of how far they'd come since their brash, unthinking younger days.

After a few moments, Devon popped the WrestleMania DVD into his player and turned up the volume. "Alright, enough of that. It's time for some Stunners and Rock Bottoms."

Chase proclaimed, "Loved that match, but I'm more looking forward to that TLC battle to near death. Jeff Hardy was a crazy man!"

They watched nearly the entire four hours while chatting, snacking and cheering along with the capacity crowd.

By the time the DVD ended, the golden sky changed the lake into an endless sea of fire. The cabin was an unmitigated mess and their highs were settling.

"Well boys, I've got about an hour before my ride picks me up," Chase said, choking back emotion, knowing this would be the last time they all would gather.

"How should we spend that last hour?" Kris wondered aloud.

"That's up to Chase," Devon added.

Without words, Chase got up to his feet with a shakiness and a few pops of his joints. He poured himself three fingers of whiskey and then slowly walked past them out to the back deck.

One by one, the men followed his lead with each of them lined up, leaning against the railing, looking out at the picture Mother Nature painted for them.

"Just like old times," Devon said quietly. "Different waist sizes, maybe, but same feeling."

Kris raised his glass in a half-salute. "Chase, you lucky son of a—You're really doing this. The first man to meet the universe on his own terms."

Chase swallowed against the lump in his throat. "I

guess so," he managed, voice soft. "Thank you, all of you, for today. Best send-off I could have asked for."

Again silent, the shared weight of time speaking without words: his friend's knowledge that the next time they'd meet, they'd be down one man.

A small blue icon blinked in Chase's peripheral vision —a discreet heads-up display from the implant near his temple. The HyperVan had arrived. He swallowed, feeling his chest tighten, then exhaled, pushing himself off of the railing with effort.

He pulled each friend into a hug, murmuring thanks and half-joking farewells. As he made his way out front, the sleek silver van shimmered against the darkening sky. Its quiet engines hummed, hovering a foot off the ground. Chase turned back to wave at his friends, all lined up on the porch with their whiskey glasses raised high.

"Well, boys," he said, voice catching in his throat, "to infinity and beyond."

The van door sealed shut with a gentle hiss, and as it rose into the evening air, Chase looked down one last time at the cabin and his old friends waving and hollering, who'd seen him through every chapter of his life. Then he felt the subtle press of acceleration, and the world below blurred out of sight, carrying him away to his final hours on Earth.

PART FOUR

Life in Death

As the sun said its final goodbye to the west, the HyperVan carrying Beth, Amy, and Ian descended onto the reception platform at Owen Industries with a near-silent hum, settling onto its magnetic rails before the doors slid open. The campus showcased humanity's technological leaps since Beth was born: tall, interlocking buildings of mirrored alloy soared skyward, each facade teeming with holographic readouts and solar panel arrays that pulsed with energy. Autonomous drones zipped by overhead, ferrying equipment between labs, while ever-present displays scrolled through planetary data and mission statuses. The air itself seemed to buzz with innovation.

Yet, for Beth, stepping out onto the smooth tarmac, all that futuristic splendour was overshadowed by the emotion of the moment. She steadied herself against the sleek HyperVan, taking a slow breath before turning to face Amy and Ian, who had accompanied her on this final ride.

Amy, seeing the emotional toll of the moment in her mother's sparkling yet saddened eyes, rushed forward to embrace her mother. Now both of their tear-lined eyes glistened with a mix of emotion as they fought for composure. "Mom," she whispered, her voice trembling. No matter how many times she'd practiced this farewell in her head, it felt impossible now that the moment had come.

Beth returned the hug, gently running her fingers through Amy's hair. Although her body felt frail from illness, her heart was determined to provide maternal devotion. "Shh, sweetheart," she managed softly. "It's going to be all right. This is where my peace continues."

Nearby, Ian held back for a moment, staring up at the campus. The imposing scale of Owen Industries—its glass bridges, neon-lit corridors, and constant activity with humans being ferried by smaller, personal HyperVan drones from floor to floor, building to building—felt surreal. *So this is where Beth will spend her last days on Earth…or in orbit*, he thought, composing himself. When he finally stepped up, he placed his hands softly on Beth's arms.

"Beth," he said quietly, mustering warmth despite the ache in his chest. "Thank you for welcoming me into your family. I promise, I'll always take care of Amy."

Beth offered him a tender smile. "I know you will, Ian. You're a good man. Just…make sure you keep an eye on her for me. She's strong, but sometimes she'll need a shoulder to lean on."

He nodded. "Don't forget to call my mom when you get up there. She's anxiously waiting to gab about your experience, and dish the gossip about what that old couple down the hall is getting up to." A shared tinge of laughter as they both wiped away the most fragile of tears.

None of them mentioned the risks of the mission outright, but the possibility loomed in every breathless sigh, every lingering look. Amy hugged her mother once more, inhaling the familiar scent she'd known all her life, one last time.

The solemn moment broke as Chase approached. There was a faint grin tugging at his lips—part kindness, part mischief—like a man who'd discovered the secret code to Oliver Owen's safe. He took in the scene: three people, obviously feeling the weight of the moment, standing before a towering edifice of steel and glass.

"All right, what is this?" he teased, spreading his arms wide. "Are we at a funeral or something? Because from my perspective, Beth and I are about to embark on the adventure of a lifetime!"

Amy couldn't help a slight giggle through her tears. Even Ian's somber expression cracked into a small smile. Chase, for all his wry humour, carried a comforting presence.

He gave Amy a quick hug. "Your mom told me all about you. I'm honoured—truly—to meet the amazing daughter she won't stop bragging about."

Amy blushed and sniffled. "She brags about me?"

Chase laughed. "You have no idea. Honestly, it's a little nauseating, but meeting you now, I get it." He said with a wink.

Then he turned to Ian, shaking his hand firmly. "I've heard about you as well, big guy. Hopelessly devoted to Beth's daughter. But a little parting advice from an old man, don't ever forget your friends," he said, voice lowering with the weight of the message, doing his best to give Ian a look that showed he meant every word. "If you do it right, they'll be there for you through everything— like mine have been for me."

Ian's gaze flickered with understanding. "Thanks, sir. I'll remember that."

Satisfied that he did his wise old man thing, Chase turned back to Beth. She was seated in the wheelchair, but her eyes glinted with determination. "No more chair," she announced, gripping the armrests. "I'm doing this on my own two feet. After tomorrow, I'll be sitting plenty."

"Mom—," Amy squealed out in concern.

Chase simply put his hand out to Amy, letting her know he had everything under control. Gallantly, he offered his arm to Beth. "May I escort you inside, Ms. Jenkins?"

Beth nodded, rising on unsteady legs. She looped her arm through his, wobbling just enough for him to give a gentle, supportive nudge. In a sweet gesture, he leaned over and gave her a soft kiss on the cheek, earning a chorus of affectionate smiles.

Amy wiped her face, stepping back to let them pass. "I love you, Mom," she said in a trembling voice.

"To the moon and back," Beth whispered, pressing her lips together to keep from sobbing. "I'll talk to you as soon as I'm in flight."

With that, Beth and Chase turned and made their way into the Owen Industries building. The automatic doors sealed behind them, and Amy and Ian were left standing outside, gripping each other's hands in quiet, tearful resolve.

It was later in the evening when Beth found a moment to catch her breath in her assigned suite. By this time, she was usually fast asleep, but the intake process and buzz of excitement in her was ever present.

Her suite was calm and sophisticated, with sleek grey walls, subtle panel lighting, furniture and bars placed all around the room for her to use as support, and a massive window overlooking the campus's illuminated walkways.

In one corner, readouts and soft holograms detailed the upcoming launch schedule, while a gentle air filtration system whispered overhead. In 2030, Owen Industries figured out how to develop a new light technology that caused zero light pollution, which allowed the stars to shine ever present overhead. *Tomorrow, I'll be amongst all of you*, she whispered to herself as a chill ran up her spine, looking out of the window.

A discreet knock startled her from her thoughts. She opened the door to find Chase, with that same mischievous grin from earlier.

She raised an eyebrow, half-amused, half-suspicious. "What are you so happy about, Mister?"

He feigned innocence, hands behind his back. "Why shouldn't I be? We're the stars of the show, you and me." He glanced around theatrically, then leaned in. "You hungry?"

Beth's stomach rumbled in response, and she laughed. "Absolutely."

From behind his back, Chase presented a dark blue rose with speckles that he found while walking the grounds. "They call this a space rose. They're only grown here," he said as she took the flower and savoured in the scent of nature. "I'm pretty sure you're not supposed to pick them but we're a little too important around here to give us any heck about it."

She smiled at him and quietly her heart fluttered a bit at his rule breaking and risky mindset. "Can I eat it?" she said with a chuckle.

"Nope, not that…but this…"

An Owen Industries staff member in a clean-cut uniform wheeled in a table bearing covered trays, silverware, candles, and a small stereo softly playing a rotation of classic rock and pop ballads from the last five decades. After lighting the candles, the staffer quietly left, leaving Beth and Chase alone with the fancy-looking spread.

Beth's eyes went wide. "You did all this?"

"Some say to live respectfully within limits, I say, Oliver Owen has no limits so neither should we," Chase said, tugging off one of the silver covers to reveal a perfectly cooked roast chicken drizzled with sauce, fresh vegetables, and crusty bread. Another cover revealed a decadent chocolate dessert. "I wish it were real chicken, but you know how hard that is to come by, so we'll have to settle for the synthetic stuff."

"I rather like it, actually."

"Well then, if you're happy, I'm happy." Chase paused for a moment and rummaged through his bag. "Oh, and turns out they don't check an old man's bag when he's the star of the show." He slipped a bottle of wine from inside, waggling his brows playfully.

Beth let out a delighted laugh. "You're terrible."

"Terrible genius," Chase corrected, uncorking the wine. "Now, shall we dine?"

They settled at the small table near the window, the glow of stars and the soft flicker of candlelight creating a comfortable and admittedly intimate atmosphere. The stereo's gentle melodies accompanied them as they talked —Beth sharing stories of Amy's childhood antics, Chase recounting many mischievous stories with his lifelong friends.

Between hearty bites and grateful sips of wine, they found themselves exchanging deeper thoughts. They laughed over the simplest memories, but tears welled at times when they touched on their upcoming mission—the final act of their lives, though neither openly said as much.

When Beth set down her third nearly empty wineglass, cheeks flushed from the alcohol, she let out a half-giddy sigh. "I haven't been this tipsy in…well, a long time. Is it weird that it feels wonderful?"

Chase clinked his glass against hers. "Not at all. We deserve to be spoiled for all life has put us through. I've been at war with my ticker for over a decade, and you have been through more than anyone should. Let's just savour everything this end of life has to offer us in this moment."

They drifted into a comfortable lull, content just to be, until *All My Love* by Coldplay played on the stereo. With the first piano chord, Beth lit up. "Oh, I *love* this song," she proclaimed.

Chase stood, sliding his chair back. "Care to dance?"

Beth hesitated, eyeing her legs. "I don't know…"

"I'll hold you tight," he said gently, extending his hand. "You have my word as a gentleman."

She cautiously let him lead her to the open space in the middle of the room. One arm slipped around her waist, the other grasped her hand. Slowly, tentatively, they began to sway. Under any other circumstance, it might have felt awkward, but in this moment it felt right.

"You know," Chase said softly into her ear, "I used to be a pretty decent singer."

Beth's smile curved against his shoulder. "Is that so?"

He chuckled, then murmured, "I wonder if I've still got it?"

"Only one way to find out," she whispered.

With the song drifting through the room, he sang along in a gentle, unpolished baritone, each note sinking deeply into her as she sunk deeper into calm. She closed her eyes, letting the melody guide her mind back to a younger self—

healthier, stronger, dancing in a carefree world. For a flicker of time, she believed she was that person again, her heart light and full of possibility.

When the song ended, they didn't even notice, swaying to silence but still keeping rhythm. Eventually, Beth lifted her cheek from his shoulder, eyes glistening. On impulse, they leaned in and shared a soft, heartfelt kiss—an affirmation of life and connection. She pulled back, breath shaky, tears threatening to spill.

"You're the first man I've kissed since my husband." She buried her face in his chest, her body trembling with the weight of so much emotion.

Chase's cheeks were flushed, and he was flustered, but he felt it important to reassure her. Cupping her face with one hand, he whispered, "I was once in love but never married," he admitted. "But if I *had* been, and something happened to me first, I'd want her to find happiness again —even if it meant moments like this with someone else."

They stood together in silence for a moment longer, holding each other, letting the world's hum fade into the background. Beth needed to get off of her feet though, so she nodded toward the bed. She wasn't ready to be alone, not yet.

They laid down atop the covers, craving closeness in the evening's hush. Beth rested her head on Chase's shoulder, draping an arm across his chest. After a few moments, she spoke softly about Ian—how his father Beck had died soon after he was born, leaving behind a book that shaped Ian's perspective on life.

"In that book," Beth explained, "Beck wrote about something called the *Harmony of Bliss*. He and his wife, Sienna, found it by simply being together, without words, until they sort of transcended everything else."

She recounted Beck's poetic description: the gentle touches, the heightened senses, the way the rest of the world simply fell away, leaving only two people in perfect harmony—breath, heartbeat, calm of mind.

"Sienna is still alive and annoyingly healthy," Beth continued. "She told me she held onto that memory like a talisman. Whenever life became too much, she revisited that feeling, grounding herself in love."

"Sounds like they had a special connection."

Beth sighed, nestling closer. "I think we touched that feeling tonight—when we danced. Even just for a little while."

Chase pressed a light kiss to her hair. "I felt it, too. Time stopped. And it was...beautiful."

A silence once again settled over them as they savoured one last night on Earth. Beth's mind slipped ahead to the mission—wondering what tomorrow would hold. "Do you ever worry about…something going wrong?" she ventured, voice soft.

He exhaled. "I did, at first. But then I remembered something you once said in an interview—that you're dying regardless, and this journey already gave you more joy than any standard hospital care could. That made sense to me. Even if things go sideways, I've had an experience that makes it all worthwhile."

Beth closed her eyes, letting relief wash over her. "I couldn't imagine doing this any other way," she whispered. "I hope it is everything Oliver thinks it will be and that the world gets to experience it."

They fell into a drowsy comfort, whispering about small things—favourite childhood foods, old songs, the feeling of summer rain. Little by little, their energy ebbed, the warmth of the wine and their emotional day finally draining them. As the lights dimmed automatically for the night cycle, they felt themselves drifting, their eyelids becoming impossibly heavy.

Tomorrow, they would begin the greatest adventure of their lives—an adventure that, by design, would be their last. But tonight, they were here, cocooned in a pocket of peace, pressing pause on the world and savouring one content moment of closeness.

In that darkened suite, as the drapes closed, blocking

out the last of the compound's light, Beth and Chase surrendered to that peace—two souls who had re-discovered a quiet harmony and dared to hold on to it, if only for this one, unprecedented and precious night.

PART FIVE

Meaning

As the drapes opened automatically at 6 a.m., sunlight filtered in through the suite's panoramic windows, bathing Beth and Chase in a warm glow as they slowly emerged from their sleep. They were still wrapped in each other's arms from the night before, and when their eyes met, twin smiles blossomed—soft, radiant, and wholly content. The in-room speakers softly played the sounds of nature as a way of lulling the room's occupants awake. Neither of them spoke for a long moment; there was no need.

Eventually, Beth laid a hand on Chase's shoulder, breathing a tired but happy sigh. He replied with a slight squeeze around her waist, pressing a light kiss to her forehead. "Morning," he whispered, his voice crackling with the latent effects of sleep.

Beth's lips curved into a playful grin. "Morning," she echoed. "I can't remember the last time I woke up so… happy."

They shared a lingering gaze, the unspoken understanding that this morning was a precious gift neither had expected to experience at this stage of their lives, or on their last day as official earthlings. It was a moment of grace before the day's monumental events began.

A booming knock cut through their serenity. Both Beth and Chase shuffled out of bed faster than either normally moved, smoothing messy hair and looking in a mirror to correct their ruffled clothing. Beth, still tugging at the hem of her sweater, opened the door to reveal Oliver standing in the hall.

He was wearing black head-to-toe, his hair messy, but it was obvious it was styled to look that way. His relaxed appearance complimented the insinuating grin curving on his face as he glanced past Beth and noticed Chase's rumpled presence in the background, along with the empty bottle of wine and equally depleted wine glasses.

"Well," Oliver said, arching a brow. "I see you two had an eventful evening. What did I miss?"

From the corner of the room, Chase called out, "A gentleman never tells." He fired off a playful wink that made Beth stifle a giggle.

"Fair enough," Oliver replied, smiling indulgently. "I'm just happy to see you both looking so joyful on…well, perhaps the most poignant day of our lives."

His gaze turned to the slept in bed before returning to Beth and Chase's content expressions. There was a glimmer in Oliver's eyes—approval, maybe even a touch of envy—that he quickly tucked behind his composed exterior.

"Care to join me for breakfast?" he asked. "We have a full day ahead, and I'd rather you not face it on empty stomachs."

They agreed, and Oliver gave them a few minutes to freshen up and change. Chase slipped away to his own room while Beth threw on a comfortable but dignified outfit. By the time they reconvened in the hallway, the clock was inching closer to *that* time.

Beth took Chase's arm once again, and they fell into step beside Oliver as they traversed the sleek corridors. Overhead, subtle LED lines guided them forward, while employees passing by paused to nod or smile. Some greeted them by name; others bowed their heads with a respect usually reserved for the most affluent. Beth felt a quiet sense of awe. *They're excited for us,* she realized. *They believe in us, in this strange, beautiful project.*

"Quite the respectful crew you have here," Chase quipped, nodding back at a young engineer who stopped to wave.

Oliver allowed a small, almost shy grin to slip. "They're a family in their own right. They know how much this program means, not just to me but to the future of end-of-life care—and, if we're bold enough, to humanity's search for answers among the stars."

They took a glass-walled elevator up to the 265th floor, a swift yet smooth ride that offered breathtaking views of the campus. In the distance, spires of other towers shimmered under the mid-morning sun. Beth and Chase were silently nervous to be travelling so high up in a little glass box, but less so than they would have been just a few months prior to their mission training simulations.

When the elevator doors parted to Oliver's private floor, he led them into his private dining room, a grand space the size of a suburban home. Its floor was constructed entirely of reinforced glass, beneath which water gently flowed—creating the impression they were walking on a crystalline lake. Cascading lights shifted through soft hues of blues, greens, and purples, reflecting up through the water and onto the dining area above. The walls were curved sheets of transparent alloy, providing a panoramic view of what felt like the entire world. Thick beams high overhead supported the structure and gave it an industrial feel, but the room somehow remained cozy, with warm, indirect lighting and tasteful, minimalist furniture.

At the center stood a sleek table set with brushed steel plates and sculpted chairs. Four robot attendants—each about five feet tall, with smooth plating and a friendly humanoid face display—glided around, checking dish temperatures and filling water glasses.

"This," Chase said, taking in the scene, "is *definitely* a step up from breakfast at my local diner."

Oliver laughed. "I do like to make an impression. We have hosted numerous charity galas up here, and I've hosted some critical diplomatic conversations at this very table."

They settled in seats previously sat in by heads of state, greeted by fresh fruit, pastries, and an array of steaming dishes. The robots, silent but efficient, delivered plates of eggs, crisp vegetables, and golden-brown waffles. One robot hovered near Chase, offering a pitcher of juice, when he raised a playful eyebrow at Oliver.

"I hear some of these advanced models give amazing massages," he said, only half joking.

Oliver shrugged and let out a boisterous laugh. "They do, actually. Go ahead—ask him."

Chase's eyes lit up. "Really?" He turned to the robot. "Mind giving these shoulders a quick tune-up, buddy?"

A moment later, the robot pivoted behind Chase's chair and extended two gentle mechanical arms, applying a soothing pressure to his shoulders. Chase closed his eyes, letting out a blissful groan that made Beth and Oliver chuckle. Despite the day's gravity, a lighthearted energy filled the room.

Plates clinked, and conversation turned to the day's schedule. Oliver explained that Beth and Chase would undergo one last medical check, a safety briefing, and final instructions regarding the press, and getting hooked up to the instrument panel.

"I'll just tell the docs to skip the alcohol and drug test," Oliver said with a smile.

"Yeah, I'd fail both those," Chase said with pride.

Beth giggled and gripped Chase's hand for a moment.

"Once you're sealed in," Oliver said softly, "you'll feel a surge of energy. That's just the instruments starting up and the supplements entering your bloodstream. Within minutes, you'll be nice and cozy. We have made one change. Your tests indicated a general anxiety about take off but not the mission itself, so with your permission, we'd like to sedate you."

Beth exhaled slowly, absorbing his words. Chase nodded, rubbing a hand across his eyes as though trying to keep himself grounded. They both nodded with acceptance of the change.

Oliver set his utensils down, gaze shifting between them. "This is your journey. I've tried to ensure it happens on your terms, no matter what arises."

They quietly acknowledged his reassurance, each

feeling the weight of what lay ahead.

Oliver continued to prepare them, but he could tell something was nagging at Beth. "What's on your mind, Beth?"

"Oh, nothing," she replied shyly.

"Beth, to get to my level, you need to be able to read people. And I'm not just talking about data inputs from our MindLink systems. I mean micro-expressions and emotions. Ask what you need to ask. Now is your only chance."

Beth ventured a question that had been tugging at her since their first interview with Oliver: "Why are you doing this? I know…bits and pieces. You want redemption for what happened years ago. You want to help. But there are less risky, less expensive ways to do good in this world."

Chase, surprised with Beth's question but clearly sharing her curiosity, raised his eyebrows and looked questioningly at their host.

Oliver leaned back, eyes fixated on the glass floor where vibrant lights danced through the water below. He seemed to ponder his response with the most careful of consideration. Finally, he spoke—his voice subdued yet steady.

"You know why this floor is the way it is?" He questioned without waiting for an answer. "You might see water and light. What is actually happening is a system called electric hydrogenesis. It's something we haven't released to the world yet in the form that exists below our feet. Basically, the water is moving in patterns that are electrified to mimic the movement of the cosmos. So when I look down at the water, I know I'm in tune with the universe."

"I have no idea what you just said," Chase called out with a belly laugh. "Sounds cool, though."

Oliver paused for another moment as patterns became evident to Beth. "Let me ask *you* both something," he said. "What do you think is the meaning of life?"

A silence fell over the table, each of them letting the question settle. Beth was the first to answer. She folded her hands on her lap, gaze far away. "I think it's the journey to find love—and once found, to give it and share it as much as possible. Romantic love, familial love, platonic love… Just love, in all its forms."

Chase nodded slowly, picking up the thread. "For me, it's about *joy*. Experiencing as much of it as we can—big or small, fleeting or long-lasting. That's why I keep my friends so close, why I traveled, why I wanted to do this mission. Joy is the thing I chase."

Oliver smiled, leaning forward. "Those answers make sense," he said kindly. "But me? I suppose I don't know.

And maybe that's *why* I'm doing this. The not knowing. I've spent my entire life gathering wealth and influence, building a technological empire. I've tasted success, heartbreak, even failure on a public stage. But none of it ever gave me…that look I saw on your faces this morning."

He smiled warmly at them, letting Beth and Chase know he knew whatever happened in that room was supposed to. "I've come close. But perhaps my meaning is to keep pushing boundaries and searching for more. Somewhere out there—beyond Earth—maybe we'll find data that redefines our place in the universe. *Why* we're the only known intelligent life, *how* we evolved this way. The more we discover, the closer I feel I might get to an answer. Or at least, closer to asking the right question."

Beth, hesitant but curious, ventured a final query: "Oliver…do you believe in God, or do you believe man can be God?"

Oliver's eyes flicked to her, thoughtful. "As a scientist and explorer, I haven't seen evidence that confirms or denies the existence of a higher power. I *want* evidence. That's part of why I fund these missions. But if I'm being honest, I can't prove or disprove anything absolutely. And that uncertainty is…difficult. As far as whether I believe man can be God, I think we need to find him or it first, and then we can assess our role in the grand scheme."

The conversation deepened, touching on the various ideas of God. They discussed how some religions see God as an omnipotent, personal being who created the universe and intervenes in human affairs; how others believe in a more pantheistic view where God *is* the universe, inseparable from nature itself. They toyed with deism—the idea that a God set the universe into motion but now remains distant—and the notion that consciousness or spirit might permeate all existence, completely interconnected like beams of light meeting. They even touched on the simulations theory swirling around scientific circles, positing that a higher intelligence could have orchestrated reality like an elaborate code.

While much of the conversation was over Chase's head, being the simpler one in the room, he chimed in about near-death experiences he'd read about, while Beth mentioned the solace many people find in prayer, spiritual meditations, or communal worship. Oliver listened intently, occasionally adding a musing remark about how quantum physics suggests there could be countless hidden dimensions or parallel realities.

"I suppose," Oliver concluded with the cock of his head and a raised eyebrow, "if I'm true to science, I have to remain open to every possibility. The evidence isn't definitive either way. So I respect people of faith and doubt alike. Maybe that's what this entire program is about, too —seeking something beyond the horizon, whether we call it God, truth, or simply the unknown."

Their unexpected, profound conversation was halted by the arrival of one of Oliver's assistants—a tall woman with an A.R. interface hovering just above her eyes. She waited for a pause, then dipped her head courteously. "Mr. Owen, Ms. Jenkins, Mr. Melnyk…it's time. Final preparations and checks will begin and the press is waiting."

Oliver looked to Beth and Chase, an apologetic yet determined expression etched across his features. "Well," he said, standing, "that's our cue. We have about eight hours until launch. Let's make them count."

Beth felt her heart pick up speed, which made her think of a cheeky jab at her interstellar companion. "Chase, if your heart is racing like mine, you might want to ask for some medication. We don't want it to give out now."

Chase rolled his eyes and laughed. "Okay sea legs. Let's get this show on the road."

Beth rose slowly from her chair, glancing one last time at the panoramic view outside the windows. The day stretched ahead, both exhilarating and terrifying. She slipped a hand into Chase's, who responded with a comforting squeeze, and together they followed Oliver out of the breathtaking dining room.

They descended again into Owen Industries' sleek corridors, the robotic attendants offering polite bows and employees nodding encouragingly. Despite the advanced technology and hints at a future they couldn't possibly understand, a very human mixture of anticipation and wonder charged the air—Beth and Chase felt it in their bones.

Eight hours, Beth thought, her chest fluttering with excitement and the slightest edge of fear. *Soon, we'll be among the stars.*

And in that moment, neither love nor joy nor answers about God seemed beyond reach. It was all part of the grandest journey yet to unfold; their interstellar funeral.

PART SIX

The Endless Expanse of Space

Gigantic steel doors—towering at least thirty feet high—slid apart slowly, with a smooth whooshing sound, revealing the heart of Owen Industries' top-secret launch facility. The space within buzzed with activity: engineers and robots hurriedly power walked across metal walkways carrying components from one station to another, and overhead cables hummed with the energy coursing through advanced quantum systems. The moment Beth, Chase, and Oliver stepped inside, the crowd turned as one—conversations paused, and even a few automated assistants swivelled lens-like heads in their direction.

Beth and Chase wore matching coveralls crisscrossed by thin cables, ports, and small devices designed to interface directly with their pods. The suits were equal parts life-support gear and communications rig, ensuring they could remain connected to Earth for as long as they stayed alive. A wave of handshakes, fist bumps, and encouraging claps on the shoulder followed them through the crowd until they reached a smaller set of doors leading to the outer launch area.

Oliver paused there, lifting a hand to direct Beth's and Chase's attention to a solemn-looking man wearing simple clerical garb. "Before the point of no return," Oliver said gently, "I wondered if you might like a prayer. Or just… a moment, if that feels right."

Beth and Chase exchanged glances. They hadn't expected a religious gesture, but neither objected; at this point, they'd take any help they could get. "Sure," Chase replied, and Beth nodded in agreement.

The minister stepped forward, bowing his head in welcome. Oliver called out for silence, and instantly every person in the facility, from the highest-ranking engineer to the humblest robotics tech, stilled. Over a discreet microphone pinned to his collar, the minister began:

"We gather here today—believers, non-believers, seekers of truth—to send off Beth Jenkins and Chase Melnyk on a journey once deemed impossible. May their path be lit by compassion, scientific marvel, and the kindness that thrives in each of us. Lord, grant them safety in the unknown. Grant Owen Industries with the clarity of mind and heart to guide this mission. And above all, let us remember we stand on the threshold of human unity and discovery. In His name we pray, Amen."

The hush remained in the prayer's wake—an interlude

of reverent calm in this, an important moment in history. Then, as if released by a quiet signal, the energy of the room surged back to life. Monitors beeped, staff resumed their tasks, and the faint whirr of robotic arms picked up once more.

Oliver offered Beth and Chase a grateful nod. "Thank you." They were about to endeavour the seemingly impossible together and he felt an overwhelming sense of gratitude that at a time when few trusted him, they did.

The next set of doors opened, and they stepped into a massive outdoor launch area with cover over the stage. Launch towers of gleaming alloy stretched for miles, flanked by rocket engines the size of city buildings. In front of them, a stage with cameras, spotlights, and dozens of microphones at the ready. A sea of reporters waited, flashing lights bursting like fireworks.

Oliver led the way. He took position at the main podium, his name glowing in holographic script behind him. Beth and Chase hung back, blinking under the assault of cameras and the electric excitement coursing through the crowd. Even the sky just beyond seemed charged with anticipation, crisscrossed by hover drones filming live footage.

"Ladies and gentlemen," Oliver began, voice carrying over the hush of the gathered press, "thank you for joining us on this historic day. We stand on the cusp of a new frontier—the Interstellar Funeral—a chance for those at life's end to choose a final journey beyond Earth's bounds." He turned, beckoning Beth and Chase forward. "It is my privilege to re-introduce our brave pioneers, Beth Jenkins and Chase Melnyk."

A roar of applause rippled across the crowd. Beth clutched Chase's hand, her heart pounding with nervous exhilaration. Together, they made their way onto the stage, again, waves of camera flashes erupting as they stood at Oliver's side. Just beyond the crowd sat two sleek, pod-like vessels mounted on a towering propulsion system— glinting silver shells that would carry the two passengers skyward.

In living rooms across the country, the footage played live. Amy, Ian, and Ian's mother Sienna watched from a comfortable couch, eyes glued to the screen. Meanwhile, Chase's group of rowdy friends sat silent, all of them leaning forward in tense excitement.

Amy placed a hand on her heart as the camera zoomed in on her mother's face. "She's holding Chase's hand. They seem…really close," she said, a note of wonder in her voice.

Sienna smirked. "I hope so. A bond like that might be just what they need up there."

At the podium, Beth gestured to Chase, then faced the world. "Over breakfast," she said, "we spoke about the meaning of life—how it might be love, or joy, or the search for something greater. We don't claim to have the answers. But we're hoping this journey might bring us all closer to them, and perhaps bring all of us closer to understanding each other's purpose."

Chase took the microphone next, offering a small wave. "Here's to finding answers, peace, and perhaps even the most beautiful of discoveries—meaning."

Oliver stepped forward to shake Chase's hand, and Beth enveloped Oliver in a warm hug. Applause thundered from onlookers, vibrating the stage. Then, a small hover-drone platform appeared, floating close enough for Beth and Chase to board. They stepped onto it, the whine of its engines harmonizing with the buzz of cameras, and soared gently above the assembly—reporters tracking every second—until they touched down near the two waiting pods.

Four Owen Industries staffers in matching jumpsuits bowed respectfully, motioning towards the elevator lifts that would get them to the pods. But before Beth and Chase climbed inside, they turned to each other. Emotions swirling in their eyes, they wrapped their arms around one another and shared a final tender, lingering kiss.

Miles away, Sienna shrieked, "You go, Beth!" while Amy's face split into a grin so wide it hurt her cheeks. Ian chuckled, squeezing Amy's hand in support. Back at the launch site, photographers captured the scene from every angle—the iconic image of two souls forging toward an otherworldly destiny.

When Beth and Chase finally broke apart, tears lined their eyes. No words were needed. Each gave a final nod to the other, then stepped onto separate lifts that whisked them upward to the pod openings.

Technicians strapped them in, hooking up countless leads and IV lines. Medical sedation would soon take hold, ensuring a calm launch despite their anxieties. The pods themselves were miniature worlds of blinking status screens, cozy seat-couches, and an array of communications technology. As the staff finished their checks, Beth felt her eyes grow heavy.

Her past flashed before her: Jesse's smile on their wedding day, cradling a newborn Amy, painting the nursery bright yellow, hosting endless family barbecues, reading bedtime stories, going for chemo treatments, receiving that fateful invitation from Oliver Owen. Next, she pictured dancing with Chase in that softly lit suite just hours ago, rediscovering the thrill of their simple kiss.

In the adjacent pod, Chase drifted into his own swirl of

memories: childhood escapades with his best friends, the smell of fresh-cut hay on the family farm, his first kiss in a high school gym, late-night star gazing with his mom, hospital stays for his failing heart, and that rejuvenating day at the cabin. And finally, Beth's laughter, her closeness, her unwavering willingness to share all of life's final joys with him.

Overhead, a robotic voice chimed that sedation would last only minutes once external connections were detached. Both Beth and Chase let themselves slip under, a soft, dreamlike calm embracing them as the pods sealed shut.

Outside, the pods were rolled several miles away across the complex's expanse of launch pads. Once positioned, the final countdown began at T-minus 2 minutes. The throngs of media, staff, and onlookers gathered at a safe distance, eyes fixed on the pods through lenses or via screens. Oliver stood on stage, heart pounding so violently he could feel it in his throat. *It's happening,* he thought. *Again.*

All at once, PTSD slammed into him so he ducked backstage to a quiet area away from onlookers. Echoes of the shuttle explosion five years back—screams, flames, the fallout and blame—rushed his mind. His vision blurred, sweat pouring down his face and neck, spattering onto the polished floor. His breath came in uneven gasps, and his legs buckled with the weight of terror. *Not again…please, not again…*

A muffled *pop* sounded from the launch pad. Oliver's eyes snapped wide open, primal panic coursing through him. Desperate to ground himself, he searched with his left hand for something to cling onto. A second pop, louder this time, indicated the rockets firing. Another wave of adrenaline spiked in Oliver's bloodstream.

In that moment, a voice crackled in his ear through his implant, calm and assured. "We have successful liftoff. All systems register normal flight."

Oliver blinked, swallowing back bile. He forced himself upright, the roar of the engines barely penetrating the layers of ballistic shielding around him. Staff in the control center erupted into short-lived cheers, hugging one another and pumping fists in the air before returning to their consoles. Shaking, Oliver inhaled a trembling breath, relief washing over him like a cool tide. A quiet, almost imperceptible smile curved his lips. *They did it,* he thought. *We did it.*

The next day's headlines blazed with praise and wonder:

REDEMPTION – featuring an image of Oliver, eyes bright with resolve.

INTERSTELLAR FUNERAL, OUT OF THIS WORLD

LOVE – with a photo capturing Beth and Chase's kiss.

Over the following months, the data stream from Beth's and Chase's pods flooded Owen Industries' servers with invaluable observations. They measured cosmic radiation levels, charted unusual solar flares, and tested communications protocols across distances that grew more uncharted each day.

Oliver made a point of speaking to them regularly. Sometimes he joined them on a three-way video link, offering updates about Earthly affairs. Beth gossiped with Sienna about the harmony of bliss she had felt dancing with Chase, giggling like two schoolgirls at their connection via the men in their lives. Chase cooked his friends back on Earth in remote-connected gaming tournaments. It took next to no time for Beth and Chase to feel comfortable in their pods and with their newfound realities.

Throughout it all, Beth and Chase continued their own conversations—sharing observations of drifting starscapes, cosmic debris, and the exquisite quiet of space. They teased each other, comforted each other, and for three months, they truly *lived*, even while knowing death was close.

But inevitably, time claimed them. Chase's fragile heart gave out first. One morning, the feed from his pod showed his vitals flatlined. Alarms on Earth flashed, and Oliver stood in silent grief as staff confirmed that Mr. Melnyk had peacefully passed.

After months of talking with Beth about the unlikely connection she had with Chase, Amy knew she had to connect with her mom and deliver the news. She also knew what that would mean for her mom. They sobbed as they spoke and said what would be their last goodbyes.

Beth's heartbreak was immediate and carried with it, the realization that space now felt empty. She recorded a poignant message for Earth and another for Oliver, thanking him for giving her hope and wonder when life had dimmed to a painful routine. And then, with tears slipping silently down her cheeks, she activated the barbiturates.

In the expanse of space, the twin pods, each occupant now gone, continued drifting deeper into the cosmos—a testament to human ambition, courage, and the boundless power of connection. Beth and Chase, though absent in body, remained forever etched into the world's memory, and the data they'd gathered would guide new generations of explorers.

Their pods would continue to send valuable data back to Earth, but their Interstellar Funeral was now complete.

PART SEVEN

Gone, But Not Forgotten

A year had passed since Beth and Chase embarked on their historic journey. In that time, Owen Industries, and in particular, Oliver Owen, dissected geopbytes of data from the mission. Their observations and their pod's data before they went offline had led to a whirlwind of discovery and advancement.

A seemingly innocuous and mundane report from Beth about the movement of her pod was dissected by Owen's team. It led to a radical breakthrough in space travel: a cost-effective, energy-efficient system that defied conventional engineering. What had been deemed impossible was now a cornerstone of the future. Beth's unintentional gift obliterated financial and logistical barriers, opening the cosmos to humanity in ways no one had dared to dream.

Just as Beth had no idea that she was providing valuable insights, Chase's continual descriptions of a strange force that caused all kinds of readings, which seemed completely normal in past space missions, aided Owen Industries to realize that science had fundamentally misunderstood black holes.

Their combined contributions catapulted space travel and the Interstellar Funeral program decades ahead of where they were before that fateful day.

Today marked the culmination of these advancements: the launch of one hundred new pods into the cosmos. Unlike the previous mission, the identities of the participants remained confidential—especially from each other, and the pods were dispatched on unique courses with individual orbits. This strategic shift aimed to prevent emotional entanglements. It wasn't that Oliver was unhappy that Beth chose to use the barbiturates, but he hoped to avoid anyone ending their mission early this time.

Beth's choice wasn't respected by everyone at first, and spawned the mantra, "A mission to redefine and evolve space travel while giving participants dignity in their final days." Oliver wanted it to be clear that the humanity of the program was just as important as the science.

That message was to be the central theme of the event today. While impressive that they were launching a hundred pods out into space and the ramifications of such a ramp up were clear, it was important that his mission to offer the ultimate chance for dignity in death be at the forefront of people's minds.

As he stood backstage in that same spot he had waited

with Beth and Chase before addressing the world, he remembered the anxiety creeping in. It was a reminder of how far he had come. Today, he exuded calm and poise. The world had forgiven his role in the ill-fated mission nearly a decade earlier and his company was celebrated for the groundbreaking mission of Interstellar Funeral.

Again, he waited by those doors for his cue as the President of the United States, who wouldn't answer his calls just a year ago, sung his praises to the pool of reporters and delegates. There was no need for a minister or a moment to himself; the science was solid and so too, was he.

"Ladies and gentlemen, the man who brought a mission to the world that encompasses love, joy, and discovery; Mr. Oliver Owen." Oliver heard the President's introduction in his implant and turned on his HUD to display his speech.

He took a deep breath, patted his suit and stepped onto the stage to exuberant applause. After shaking hands with the President and waving to the crowd and cameras, he took a moment to absorb the scene.

"Today, we take the next monumental step forward in science and humanity," Oliver began, his voice steady and resonant. "The Interstellar Funeral mission continues today as we launch one hundred pods, each embarking on its own unique orbit, each with distinct goals in mind. This mission is powered by the groundbreaking science discovered through Chase and Beth's mission in the original pods, now aptly named Love and Joy, and now thanks to that mission, relics by today's standards."

The crowd responded with further applause, their faces alight with hope and excitement. Oliver paused once again, allowing a break in his message before setting Beth's last transmission to take center stage.

"It has been just over a year since we stood here last, sending two beloved people, Beth and Chase on their one-way mission to the great beyond," he continued. "Today, I have the honour of sharing something deeply personal—Beth's final transmission to the world."

A holographic screen flickered to life behind him, displaying Beth's message. Her words, though simple, carried the weight of her journey and the mission's true purpose.

Beth's Message to the World:

"My whole life has been fairly unremarkable to anyone that has a sense of adventure or loves a good thrill—until now. This journey has given me enough excitement to fill up my sixty-plus years on this planet.

Before this, I lived for love, so I will end with love. I have no doubt that Oliver Owen will find a way to launch many more people into space and give them all a wondrous and peaceful ending. So this is the message I would like the next travellers to hear.

If you're leaving Earth now and you've left anything unsaid to anyone, use the comms system to say it. Share your message with love and hope and don't let the inevitable negativity of this world win the day.

If anything, this mission proves something very important. There is always more to the story than we can first see. So why die on the hill you feel passionate about? Instead, die on the hill of interstellar love.

And to everyone else, I leave you with this final thought: Hold difference in your heart, because for generations difference has been a catalyst for war, but it could just as easily be a catalyst for love, joy...and meaning. Welcome difference and embrace it. While Oliver will advance our species scientifically, that's how we can all advance our species in the most holistic of ways.

I love you all, Beth."

Oliver allowed Beth's poignant words to sink in— especially for the hundred passengers about to embark on their mission—before addressing the crowd again. You could almost hear the thoughts of those in attendance.

"Beth's message is a beacon of love, hope, and unity. It embodies the very spirit of this mission—exploring the unknown while cherishing the bonds that tie us together. Her and Chase's contributions to science are now well documented. This program's contributions to the world are now well documented. What is lesser known is my appreciation. I am so incredibly thankful that you—all of you—have allowed me the trust to once again change the world. Through my darkest days, I founded this program. If you're going through dark times right now, know that the light will shine for you once again. Thank you."

Wasting no time, he gave the command to commence the launch sequence. Unlike the previous mission, the pods were not wheeled out individually. Instead, they began to move down the expansive runway on their own power, gaining speed with each passing second. The sight was mesmerizing—one hundred pods soaring into the sky, their sleek designs cutting through the clouds with precision. The pods, each lifted off in a synchronized dance, breaking formation to establish their individual orbits. It was an impressive sight, the culmination of a year of relentless effort and unwavering dedication.

Oliver looked to the sky from the stage waiting to hear those words that saved him last time. "We have successful liftoff. All systems register normal flight." He closed his eyes, let his shoulders fall, and then looked down at the podium where a picture of him, Beth and Chase lay flat as a reminder of why he was here.

As the crowd gazed upward in awe, Oliver felt a surge of pride and hope. He scanned the faces before him, soaking in their excitement that radiated from every individual present. They looked to the sky with wonder. They looked to the sky with awe. Many pointed and drew the path of individual pods with their finger as photographers and videographers as well as the drones that followed the ships into the clouds tried to get iconic shots that would define the moment.

The President once again approached Oliver and shook his hand. "Great job, Oliver. Stellar. So happy to be a part of this program. Next time, let's launch a thousand pods!"

Oliver smiled at his fair-weather *friend*. Although he didn't trust the man or particularly like him, he replied with confidence, "Two thousand…a month!"

Laughing and slapping him on the back, the President walked off the stage to glad hand the delegates in the audience who also had their eyes locked to the sky.

Oliver once again scanned the audience before leaving the stage but as he turned his eyes fell upon two figures at the back of the crowd—a man and a woman, both appearing to be in their twenties. They were, from what he could tell, the only people not looking up. Instead, they were looking him right in the eyes. The woman smiled at him while the man gave him a thumbs up.

Oliver felt an inexplicable kinship with them, a pull that drew him in despite not being able to place them but also understanding somehow that they were familiar. Then he had a thought—an impossible thought. Doubt gnawed at his mind—*could this be possible?* He struggled to process the wild ideas that his brain was conjuring up.

The couple continued to smile warmly at him before approaching the barricades in front of the stage. They spoke briefly with a security guard, who looked up at Oliver for instruction. He motioned for them to be let through.

As they walked up onto the stage, Oliver's mind finally accepted the surreal reality of what he was witnessing. The man and woman stood before him, hand in hand, their presence exuding a calm and unwavering confidence that brought Oliver both a sense of unease and contentment.

He sputtered out two words, his voice barely audible, hidden under disbelief and reverence. "Beth? Chase?"

The woman replied softly, her energy beaming with the same love that had defined her the last time they had spoken. "Hello, Oliver. We have a lot to talk about."

Oliver felt his heart race, emotions swirling within him —disbelief, joy, confusion, and an overwhelming sense of déjà vu. Somehow, Beth and Chase had returned from the dead and not just that, returned to Earth. Not just returned, but they looked younger and healthy. Beth had the glow of youth and vitality, while Chase appeared strong and energetic—a stark contrast to the frailty that had characterized their final days a year ago.

With the world fixated on the ships sailing into space for one hundred interstellar funerals, no one noticed the three of them standing on stage. Oliver, shell-shocked, struggling to comprehend what was happening. Beth and Chase, with their newfound vigour and radiant calm, faced him with eyes that held stories beyond earthly explanation. Three people meeting again with ramifications that were beyond anything Oliver had ever imagined.

Beth reached out to Oliver for a hug, and then Chase joined them. Time stopped. When he finally let go of them he asked, "How?"

Chase placed a reassuring hand on Oliver's shoulder. "We have a message for you. Once you hear it, everything will become clear."

Quintessence, Book 1: The Last First Date is available now on Amazon.

Quintessence Book 2: Beck's Book, an emotional tale about Beck's determination to guide Ian through the most daunting aspects of life, even after he's gone, will be available December 2025.

About the Author

Jay Hall is an English author writing novels based in genre, such as Contemporary Romance, but with social commentary and exploration of human condition. He has written for various publications and this is to be considered his first work as a professional writer.

When Jay isn't obsessing over dialogue tags and making expressions in the mirror to figure out how they should be described, you can find him in the podcast studio, producing Better, or taking some sort of risk that you'd probably consider unnecessary. His TBR list is massive and his dream of having one of his books turned into a movie continues.

Book Club Questions

If you belong to a book club, may I recommend these conversation points to discuss Interstellar Funeral.

1. What did you like best about this book?

2. What did you like least about this book?

3. What other books did this remind you of?

4. Which characters in the book did you like best?

5. Which characters did you like least?

6. If you were making a movie of this book, who would you cast?

7. Share a favourite quote from the book. Why did this quote stand out?

8. Would you read another book by this author? Why or why not?

9. What feelings did this book evoke for you?

10. What did you think of the book's length? What would you cut or extend?

11. What songs does this book make you think of? Create a playlist together!

12. Which character in the book would you most like to meet?

13. Which places in the book would you most like to visit?

14. What do you think of the book's title? What other title might you choose?

15. What do you think of the book's cover?

16. What do you think the author's purpose was in writing this book?

17. How original and unique was this book?

18. What character's perspective would you like to hear the book through?

19. What artist would you choose to illustrate this book?

20. Did this book seem realistic?

21. How well do you think the author built the world in the book?

22. Did the characters seem believable to you?

23. Who did the characters remind you of?

24. Did the book's pace seem too fast/too slow/just right?

25. If you wrote fanfic about this book, what story would you want to tell?

26. Email me? Ask me a post-read question: bettercalljayhall@gmail.com.

www.ingramcontent.com/pod-product-compliance
Lightning Source LLC
Chambersburg PA
CBHW070532130626
46555CB00003B/1388